This igloo book belongs to:

....

igloobooks

Written by Stephanie Moss
Illustrated by Emanuela Mannello

Designed by Alex Alexandrou
Edited by Caroline Richards

An imprint of Igloo Books Group,
part of Bonnier Books UK
bonnierbooks.co.uk

Published in 2019
by Igloo Books Ltd, Cottage Farm
Sywell, NN6 0BJ

Manufactured in China. GOL002 0519
10 9 8 7 6 5 4 3 2 1

Library of Congress Cataloging-in-Publication
Data is available upon request.

ISBN 978-1-83852-527-9
IglooBooks.com
bonnierbooks.co.uk

Unicorn Kisses

igloobooks

Eva just loved unicorns. She thought about them all day long.
If anyone said they weren't real, she was sure that they were wrong.

Unicorn toys in her bedroom were in piles ten feet high.

And she longed to see one flying gracefully up in the sky.

Eva had a pretty pony that she played with every day.
She'd pretend she was a unicorn. "Fly, Sparkle, fly," she'd say.

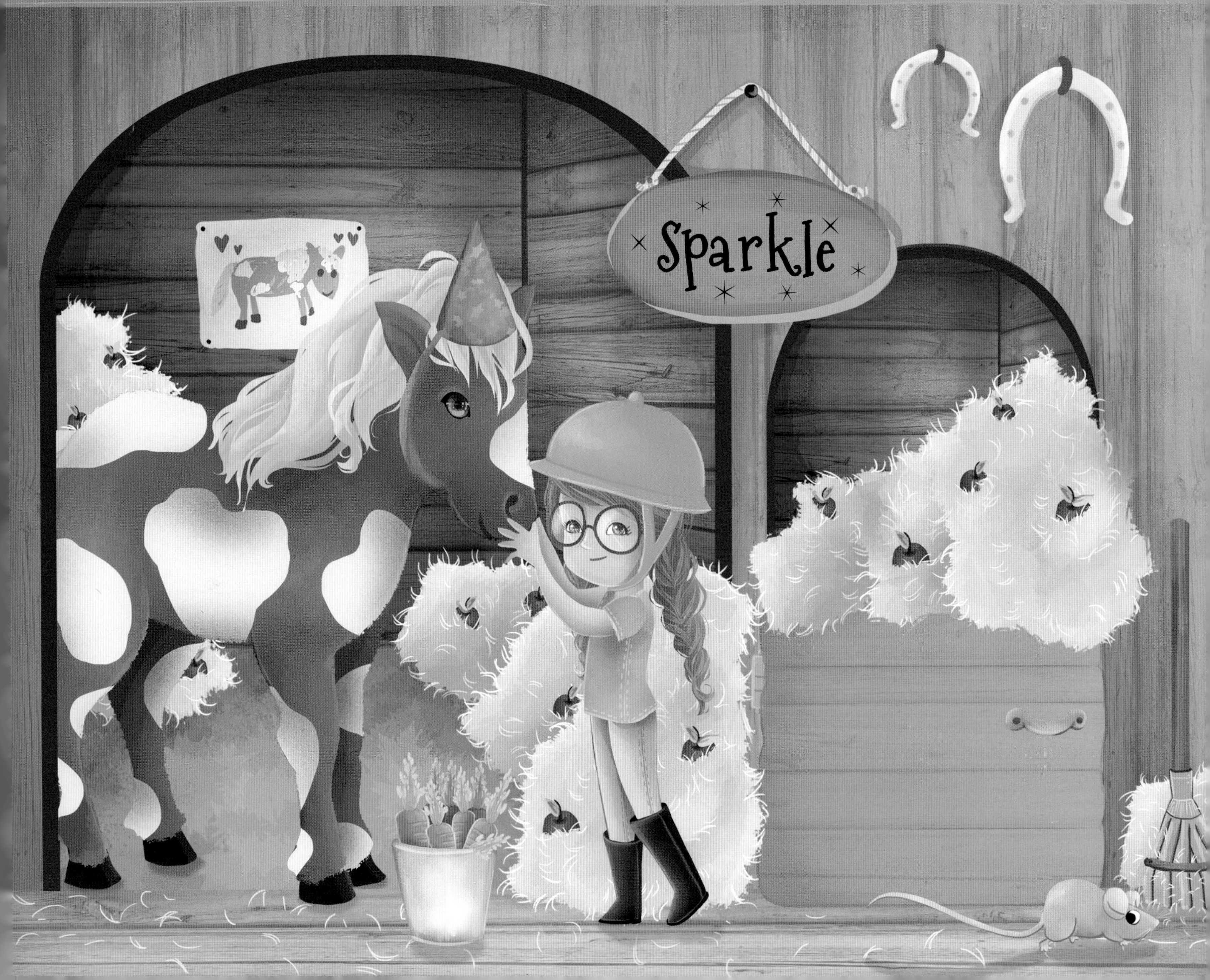
Sparkle

"But unicorns don't exist," all Eva's friends giggled with glee.

"Come to my special party," she said. "Just you wait and see!"

The stables were all decorated in pink, purple, and green.
It was the most enchanting party that Eva had ever seen!

Before her friends arrived,
Eva kissed Sparkle's soft,
warm head.

"I wish you REALLY
were a unicorn,"
she closed her eyes and said.

Then all of a sudden,
her pony began to glow.
Wings and a horn
appeared, and rainbow
hair started to grow!

The stunning unicorn
was far beyond her
wildest dreams.
She twinkled like the
stars and looked as
pretty as moonbeams.

Sparkle's voice was soft and gentle.
She said, "Let's fly off on the breeze!"
Eva climbed up on her back, as she cried,
"WOO-HOO! WHEE! Yes, please!"

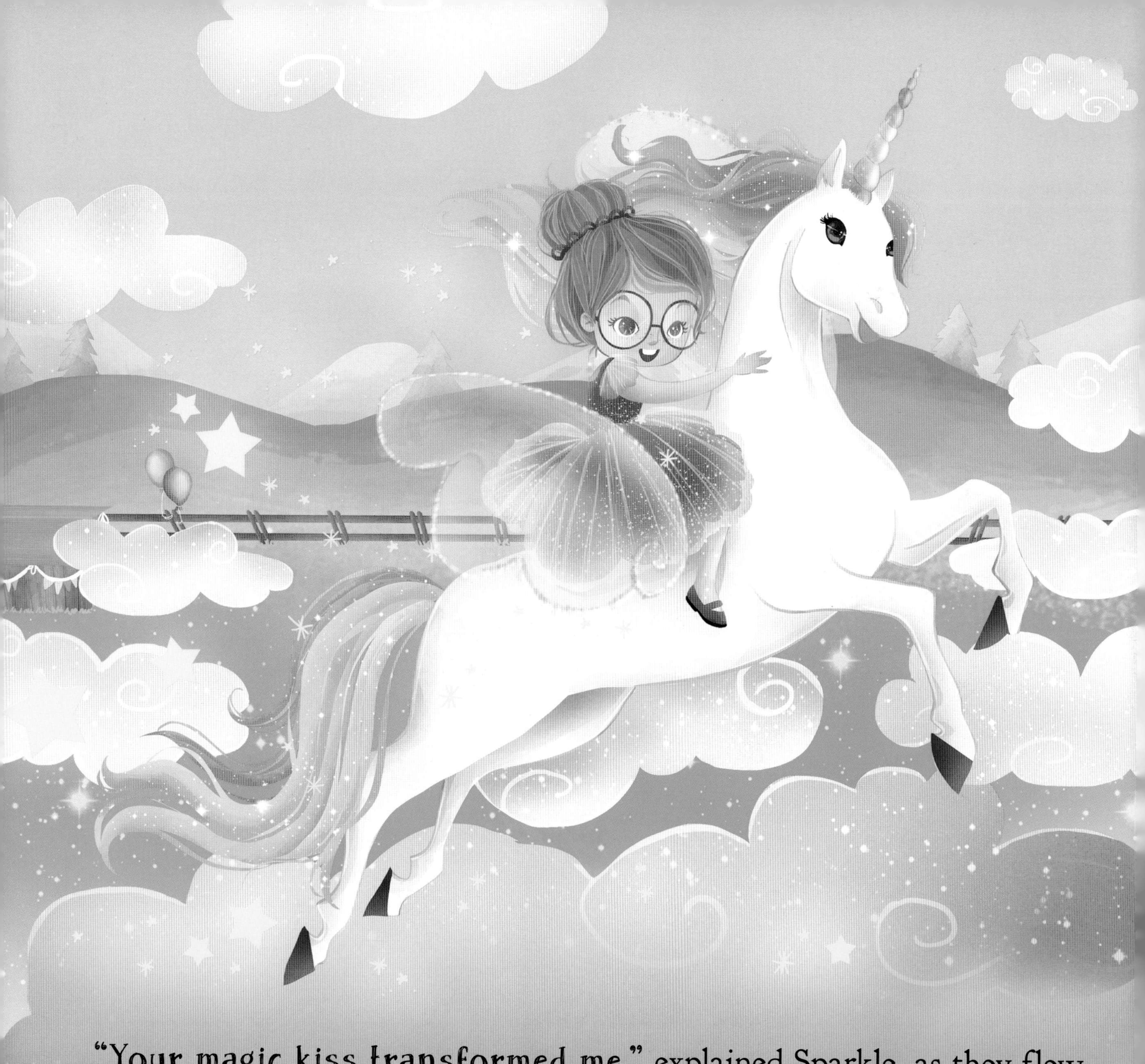

"Your magic kiss transformed me," explained Sparkle, as they flew. "Most people don't believe in us. Most people aren't like you."

They glided past a rainbow on marshmallow clouds of white.
Then far off in the distance, something gleamed in the sunlight.

Eva saw a magic palace and,
as she looked all around,
Sparkle shook her mane and smiled,
landing gently on the ground.

The other unicorns were playing at the forest waterfall.
Eva thought they were so beautiful she had to meet them all!

"I'm Shimmer,"
said one unicorn.
"I'm Moonshine,"
said one more.

Their beauty was like nothing she had ever seen before.

To celebrate her visit, they brought her treats of every kind.

There were so many things to choose from, but Eva didn't mind!

"I hope my party is this good," she said.

"We'd all have so much fun."

With just one swish of Sparkle's tail,

Eva's special wish was done.

When it was time to go, Sparkle flew Eva through the stars. "What a magical adventure," said Eva, "and it's all ours."

Back home, she kissed Sparkle and said, "Thank you," in her ear.

Sparkle turned back into a pony, then Eva saw her friends appear.

"You were right all along," they said.
"This party is the best. If only unicorns were real.
Then we'd really be impressed!"

Eva gave a secret smile and she winked at Sparkle, too.

"You just have to believe," she said.

"Then your wish will come true."

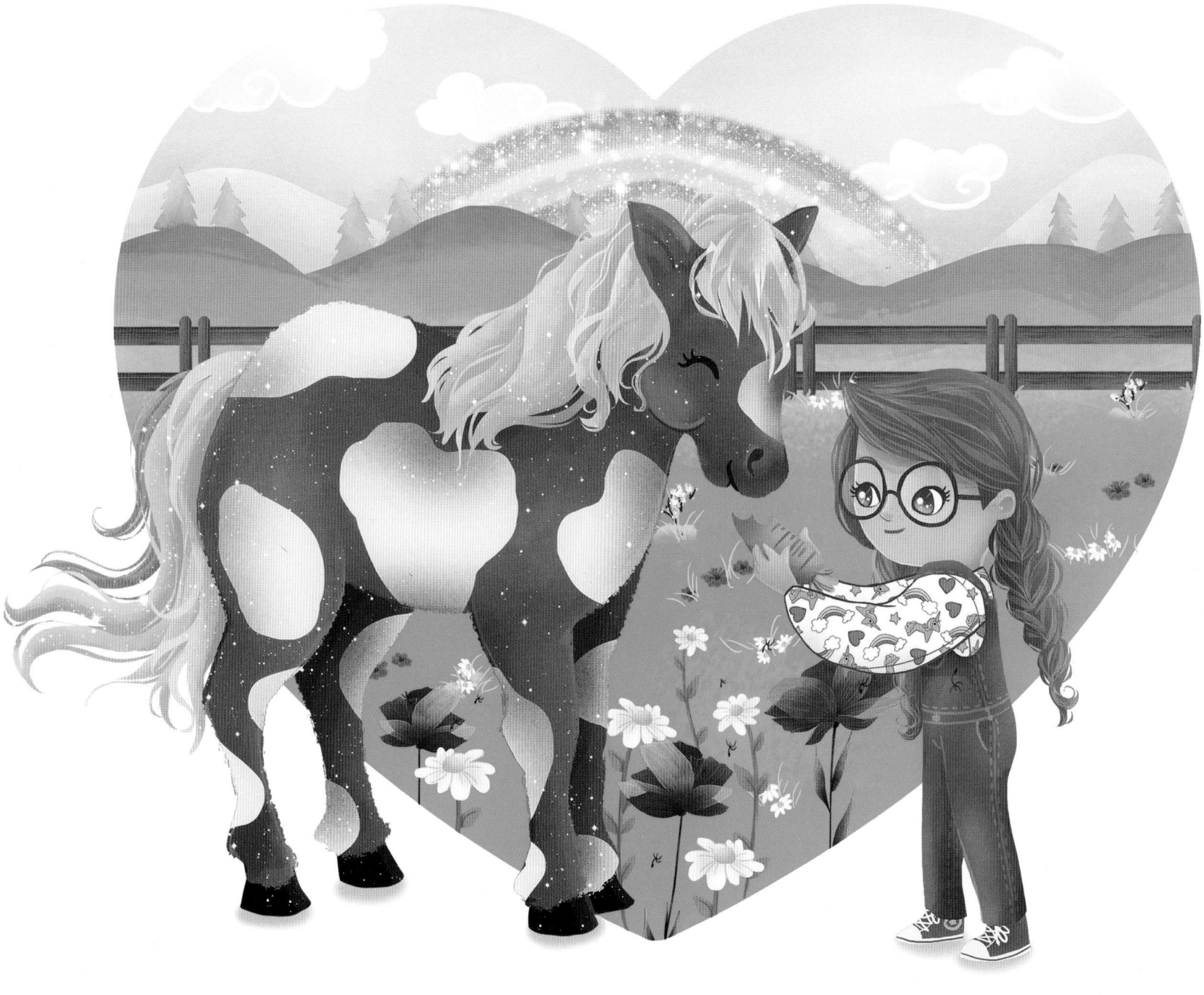